SHE REMEMBERED

For the girl who is just beginning

Kendra Tamika

Remember Her Publishing

She Remembered

Published by Remember Her Publishing

ISBN: 979-8-9954705-4-0

LCCN: 2026910023

First Edition

Printed in the United States of America

She Remembered is part of the Remember Her Girls Series published by Remember Her Publishing.

For my daughter.

You are Nova.
You have always been Nova.

And for every girl who needs to see herself in a story
the girl who is just beginning,
the girl who is finding her way back,
the girl who forgot for a little while
and is learning to remember.

This book is proof that your story matters.
That your voice matters.
That you matter.

Remember her.
She is you.
And she is extraordinary.

TABLE OF CONTENTS

A NOTE FROM THE AUTHOR

This book was written for my daughter.

The girl who came into this world fighting before she ever took her first breath. The girl who wakes up every morning with more joy than most people carry in a week. The girl who is unapologetic about who she is in every space she enters and has taught me more about remembering myself than anything else ever has.

Nova is for her.

And Nova is for you.

For the girl who is just beginning. For the girl who is in the middle of forgetting. For the girl who is finding her way back.

You were born knowing exactly who you are.

The world is going to try to make you forget.

Your only job is to remember.

With love,

Kendra Tamika

CHAPTER 1

The Day It All Began

Nova knew things.

She knew that pink was the color of her favorite everything. She knew that rocks had personalities if you looked at them long enough. She knew that the best oatmeal in the entire world had cinnamon, nutmeg, ginger, and vanilla all together in one bowl.

And she knew, in the deep quiet place inside her where the truest things lived, that she was exactly who she was supposed to be.

She had always known.

Nova's locs were small and beautiful and they did whatever they wanted.

Sometimes they fell forward over her shoulders like they were trying to see what she was looking at. Sometimes they stood up a little at the top like they had somewhere important to be. Sometimes Mama put them in two big puffs with bows that matched her dress and Nova would look in the mirror and think: Yes. That is me.

She liked being her.

She had always liked being her.

The building was bigger than she remembered buildings being.

She had been in public school before, second grade, briefly, before the decision was made to bring her home and do things differently, but that building had felt like a building. This one felt like a small city. The hallways stretched in every direction from the main entrance, and they were full, completely, overwhelmingly, loudly full, of kids who all seemed to know exactly where they were going and exactly what they were doing and exactly who they were doing it with.

Nova stood just inside the front doors between her mom and her dad and took it all in.

The sound hit first. It was not bad sound exactly, it was the sound of a hundred different conversations happening at the same time, lockers opening and closing, sneakers squeaking on the polished floor, someone laughing very loudly somewhere to the left, music coming faintly from somewhere she could not identify. It was a lot. It was a lot all at once.

Her hand moved toward her backpack strap automatically. The headphones were in the front pocket. She had packed them herself last night after her mom suggested it and she had been grateful for the suggestion even though she had initially said she probably would not need them.

She might need them.

That was when she saw the art.

It was on the wall to the right of the entrance, a long mural that stretched nearly the entire length of the hallway. In the center of the mural in large letters that someone had clearly taken great care with were the words:

YOU BELONG HERE.

Nova stared at it for a moment.

Something in her chest loosened just slightly.

The homeroom was a good sized classroom, windows along one wall letting in the morning light, desks arranged in a loose cluster rather than perfect rows which Nova immediately liked because perfect rows felt like you were supposed to be identical and she had never been interested in being identical.

There were posters on the walls and a bookshelf in the corner and a whiteboard at the front where someone had written Welcome to 6th Grade, Ms. Carter in green marker with a small star at the end.

Nova saw the star and decided immediately that she liked Ms. Carter.

A girl walked in.

She was about Nova's height, maybe half an inch shorter, with deep brown skin that was almost exactly the same shade as Nova's own and hair that Nova immediately and involuntarily noticed. Long natural curls, dark as night, thick and glossy, falling past her shoulders in the kind of effortless way that made it look like her hair had simply decided to be magnificent and followed through on that decision every single day.

She had a bright yellow backpack and a pencil case covered in stickers and an expression on her face that Nova recognized immediately because she saw it in her mirror every morning.

Curious. Excited. A little bit nervous. Trying not to show the nervous part.

Their eyes met.

The girl smiled first. It was a good smile, genuine, no performance in it.

"Hi," she said. She walked over like they were already friends. "I'm Simone. I think you might be in my homeroom."

"Nova," Nova said, and she stuck out her hand because that was what you did when you met someone new.

Simone looked at the hand for approximately half a second and then shook it, which made them both smile.

"I love your backpack," Simone said.

"Thank you," Nova said. "I love your hair."

"Thank you," Simone said. And then: "Your locs are really pretty."

Nova touched one of her locs self-consciously and then stopped touching it because she was not self-conscious about her locs, she loved her locs, and there was no reason to act otherwise.

“Thanks,” she said. “I’ve been growing them for four years.”

“Four years,” Simone repeated, clearly impressed. “That’s commitment.”

“My nana says commitment is how you show love,” Nova said.

Simone nodded thoughtfully. “Your nana sounds smart.”

“She really is,” Nova agreed.

That was the moment it happened.

It came out of nowhere the way these things always did, not announced, not gradual, just suddenly present. One moment Nova was standing in the homeroom talking to this girl Simone who seemed genuinely nice and the next moment the excitement of the morning, the building, the mural, the art on the walls, the new face smiling at her, the smell of the classroom, the sound of more kids arriving in the hallway outside, it all arrived in her body at the same time like a wave she had not seen coming.

Her hands came up.

She started to rock.

It was not something she decided to do. It never was. It was just what her body did when the world got to be a lot and needed somewhere to put the extra, the extra sensation, the extra input, the extra everything that her nervous system processed at a volume that other people’s did not seem to. Rocking was the pressure valve. The release. The way her body said I’ve got this, just give me a second.

She rocked and her hands moved in the small specific pattern they always moved in when she was coming back to herself.

She was in it for maybe thirty seconds.

When she came back, when the wave settled and the world came back into focus at a manageable volume, the first thing she saw was Simone's face.

Simone was not being unkind. Nova wanted to be clear about that even in her own head. Simone's face was not mean. It was just, uncertain. Slightly wide-eyed. The expression of someone who had not seen that before and did not know what it meant and was trying to figure out if they should say something or pretend they had not noticed or ask a question.

"Sorry," Nova said automatically, and then immediately wished she had not said sorry because she had nothing to apologize for and her mom had told her that a thousand times. "I stim sometimes. When I get excited or overwhelmed. It's just how my brain works."

Simone blinked. And then her face did something that Nova had not expected.

It relaxed.

"Oh," she said simply. "Okay." And then: "My little brother does something similar. He hums. Like, constantly. My mom says it's his superpower."

Nova looked at her.

"Your mom sounds smart too," she said.

Simone laughed. It was a good laugh. The kind that meant she actually found something funny.

"She tries," Simone said.

The bell rang. Ms. Carter walked in carrying a coffee mug and a stack of papers and the star on the whiteboard suddenly felt like even more of a good sign than it had before.

"Good morning," Ms. Carter said, looking around the room at the students settling into seats. She had warm eyes and natural hair and the kind of presence that made you feel like she was actually going to pay attention to you specifically not just the class generally. "Welcome to sixth grade. I'm Ms. Carter. This is homeroom. And before we do anything else I want everyone to read what it says on that wall in the hallway."

A few students looked confused.

"You belong here," Nova said quietly.

Ms. Carter looked at her across the room.

"Exactly," she said. And smiled. "Every single one of you. You belong here."

Lunch was the social Olympics of middle school and nobody had given Nova a training schedule.

She spotted Simone near the middle of the room. Simone was at a table with two other girls. They were both looking at a phone together and laughing at something on the screen. One of them had long bone straight hair and a very put-together outfit. The other had her hair in a high ponytail and the kind of easy confidence that came from knowing everyone in the room.

Nova recognized the type even if she did not know the specific people. These were the girls who had grown up in this neighborhood. Who had known each other since they were in diapers probably.

Simone looked up and saw Nova at the door.

She waved.

Nova crossed the cafeteria and slid into the empty seat across from Simone like it was perfectly natural to do so.

"Nova," Simone said. "This is Brianna and Kayla."

"Hey," said Brianna, the put-together one, with the kind of hey that was not unfriendly but was also not particularly warm.

"Hi," said Kayla, and her eyes moved briefly over Nova, the pink dress, the locs with their bows, the sparkly backpack currently being unzipped to reveal a Nutella sandwich, a water canteen, Cheez-Its, and a sketchbook.

Nova set her sketchbook on the table beside her tray.

“You draw?” Brianna asked, nodding at it.

“Manga mostly,” Nova said. “I’m working on a character right now. I’ve been trying to get the eyes right for three weeks.”

“Can I see?”

Nova slid the sketchbook across. Brianna opened it and looked at the drawing and her face did something genuine, something that briefly bypassed whatever social performance she was running and just responded honestly.

“This is really good,” she said. And she meant it.

“Thank you,” Nova said.

She took a bite of her Nutella sandwich and picked up her pencil and started adding detail to the background of the drawing while she ate because that was just what she did and she saw no reason to do otherwise.

Under the table she could feel her foot starting to tap, the low level stim that meant she was comfortable enough to be herself but aware enough of the space to keep it small. She let it tap. Nobody could see it under the table. But more importantly she was not doing it for them. She was doing it for herself because it helped her think.

So her foot tapped.

Nova Cole.

Twelve years old.

Artist. Creator. Collector of rocks and truths and things worth remembering.

On her first day of middle school.

Exactly who she was.

She Remembered — Reflection

◆ When did you first walk into a new place and feel both excited and nervous at the same time? What helped you get through it?

◆ Have you ever apologized for something that was not actually wrong, just different? Why do you think you said sorry?

◆ Nova's stim is the way her body takes care of itself. What does your body do when you need to calm down or feel better?

◆ What is the thing about you that makes you most yourself, the thing you would never want to hide?

> *You belong exactly where you are. Not the adjusted version of you. Not the quieter or smaller or more convenient version. The full version. The real one. The one with the sketchbook and the bows and the foot that taps under the table. That version belongs everywhere she goes.*

Remember Her

The girl who walks into a new room carrying everything she is, that is not bravery. That is just Nova. That is just you. You were born knowing exactly who you are. Never forget it.

CHAPTER 2

The Good Girl Rules

Nobody told you the rules.

That was the thing Nova had not expected about middle school. In every movie she had ever watched and every book she had ever read about starting a new school there was always a moment where somebody sat the new girl down and explained how things worked. Who sat where. Who liked who. What you were supposed to care about and what you were definitely supposed to pretend you did not care about even if you actually did.

Nobody did that.

You were just supposed to know.

Nova did not know.

But she was paying attention.

Their friendship had started with anime and stayed there long enough to become something real.

It turned out Simone knew every single episode of Glitter Force. Not casually knew, knew knew. Favorite character knew. Could recite specific scenes knew. Had opinions about which transformation sequence was the best and was prepared to defend those opinions at length knew. Nova had met exactly zero people her age who could match her on Glitter Force and the discovery that Simone was one of them felt like finding a particular kind of rare rock, the kind you pick up and immediately know is special even before you can explain why.

They talked about their favorite characters at lunch. They debated which episodes were the best. They drew their favorite characters side by side in their sketchbooks, Simone's style looser and more gestural, Nova's more precise and detail-oriented, and compared them and found that their different approaches made the characters look like they actually existed in the same world.

They talked about their families too. About being only children. About the particular loneliness of not having a built-in person to talk to when things felt heavy.

"It's like," Simone said one afternoon, looking at her drawing, "you're never actually alone but sometimes you feel alone anyway."

"Yes," Nova said immediately. Because that was exactly it.

They both loved pink. They both had a thing for collecting, Simone collected stickers the way Nova collected rocks. They were both, underneath everything, kind girls trying to figure out who they were in a world that had a lot of opinions about who they should be instead.

Nova had not had a friend like this before.

Brianna and Kayla had always been at the edges of things.

They were in some of the same classes and they sat at the same lunch table and they were not unkind exactly. Brianna had looked at Nova's drawings three more times since the first day and meant it each time when she said they were good. Kayla was funny in the sharp precise way that some people were funny, able to read a room and find the thing that would get the laugh.

They were just, different. From Nova and Simone both. They operated by a set of rules that Nova had been observing all semester and still had not fully decoded. Rules about what was cool and what was not. About what you were supposed to care about and how much. About how you were supposed to talk and move and present yourself in the particular social theater of sixth grade.

Nova did not naturally follow those rules.

But she noticed them. She always noticed everything.

The first moment things shifted was so small she almost talked herself out of having seen it at all.

It was a Thursday. Lunch. The four of them at their usual table. Kayla was telling a story about something that had happened in PE that morning and it was the kind of story that was funny mostly because of the way Kayla told it.

Kayla reached the punchline.

Brianna laughed. Loud and genuine.

And Simone –

Simone laughed too.

But it was not her regular laugh.

Nova knew Simone's regular laugh. She had heard it approximately a thousand times over the past few months. It was a real laugh, it started somewhere in her chest and arrived in the room before Simone had fully decided to let it out.

This was not that laugh.

This was a different sound. Shorter. More deliberate. The laugh of someone who had decided that laughing was the correct response to this moment and had produced a laugh accordingly.

Nova looked at Simone.

Simone was already looking back at Brianna, still smiling, saying something about PE, fully engaged in the conversation.

Nova looked down at her sketchbook.

She kept drawing.

She filed it away in the quiet careful part of her where all the small important things went to wait.

The hallway moment happened between classes.

Nova was walking with Simone, Brianna, and Kayla when her hands started their thing. Not the big full stim. Just the small version. Fingers moving in their private pattern at her sides while her brain processed the conversation and the hallway noise.

Her hand caught the edge of Kayla's binder.

It was not a hard collision. The binder tilted. Kayla grabbed it before it fell. Nothing actually happened.

But Kayla's face did something.

"Nova." Her voice was sharp. "Can you just —" she gestured vaguely at Nova's hands. "Why are you always doing that? You're always moving, you're always —" she seemed to be searching for the word and settled on one that landed flat and hard and wrong. "— weird."

The hallway kept moving around them.

Simone went slightly still.

Nova opened her mouth.

She had things to say. She knew what she wanted to say, the same clear matter-of-fact explanation she had given Simone on the first day. She knew the words. They were right there.

But something happened between knowing them and saying them.

Maybe it was Simone's stillness. Maybe it was the way Brianna was looking at her sideways. Maybe it was the particular vulnerability of standing in a middle school hallway with people moving all around you and someone using the word weird about the thing your own body did automatically to help itself survive.

She started to speak.

"I - I just - I -"

The stutter came without warning the way it sometimes did when her nervous system was running too many things at once.

"Okay," Kayla said. Not meaning to be cruel probably. But her tone had that particular quality of someone who had run out of patience. "We get it, Nova. Come on."

She turned and walked. Brianna followed.

Simone looked at Nova for a moment.

Nova looked back.

There was something in Simone's face that looked like it wanted to say something. An apology maybe.

But the moment passed.

"Come on," Simone said instead, softer than Kayla had said it.

And she followed them down the hallway.

Nova stood there for three seconds.

Then she followed too.

She Remembered — Reflection

- ◆ Have you ever been in a moment where you knew what you wanted to say but something stopped you from saying it? What was that something?
- ◆ What does it feel like in your body when someone says something unkind about a part of you that you cannot change?
- ◆ Nova noticed that Simone's laugh sounded different. She is always paying attention. What is something you have noticed about a friendship that you have not said out loud yet?
- ◆ What would you have said to Kayla in that hallway if you had found the words?

> *The things that make you different are not flaws. They are the specific signature of your specific brain. Nobody gets to make you feel ashamed of the way your body takes care of itself. Nobody. Not in a hallway, not anywhere, not ever.*

Remember Her

The girl who noticed everything and filed it away carefully was not being weak in that hallway. She was being human. And the moment she finds her voice, she is going to use it.

CHAPTER 3

The Weight She Carried

The first semester of sixth grade passed the way good things sometimes did, quickly and warmly and in a way that made you realize only later how much you had been enjoying it while it was happening.

Nova had not expected to love middle school.

She had expected to survive it. To navigate it the way she navigated most new things, carefully, curiously, with her headphones in her backpack as backup and her sketchbook as her anchor. She had expected it to be fine. Maybe even good on the better days.

She had not expected Simone.

But something had been changing since the hallway.

Not all at once. Not dramatically. Just slowly and quietly the way things changed when you were paying attention to them.

Simone had been spending more time with Brianna and Kayla.

Not instead of Nova. Not obviously. Just, more. A lunch where Simone sat slightly closer to Brianna than to Nova. A conversation where Simone laughed at something Kayla said and the laugh sounded slightly different from her real one. A moment where Nova said something enthusiastic about something she loved and Simone glanced at Brianna before responding.

Nova noticed all of it.

She filed it away.

She told herself it was nothing.

The weight she was carrying did not have a name yet.

It was not sadness exactly. Not anger. Something quieter than both of those things and somehow heavier. The particular weight of a moment where something you had been almost-knowing for a long time finally becomes completely known. Where the story you have been telling yourself, it's fine, she's still my friend, we're still okay, runs out of room to exist.

She was also carrying something else.

The sketchbook had been staying in her bag more often lately.

Not because she had made a rule about it. It had just become the new normal the way things became normal when you did them enough times without questioning them. Her hand still moved toward her bag sometimes, muscle memory reaching for the thing that helped her think, and then stopped. Redirected.

She was aware this was happening.

She told herself it was practical. That pulling out her sketchbook at the lunch table made Kayla look at her a certain way and she did not want to deal with that look. That it was just for now. That she would start bringing it out again when things felt more settled.

She believed this.

Mostly.

Reina noticed before Nova said a word.

That was the thing about mothers. They did not always need words. They needed eyes. And Reina had been watching her daughter since the day she came into this world and she knew every version of Nova's face.

This was the quiet one. The slightly smaller one. The one where Nova was still smiling, because Nova was always smiling, but the smile was doing a job instead of just existing.

Reina set down what she was doing.

She sat beside Nova on the bed.

And before a single word passed between them she opened her arms and pulled her daughter in.

Just that. Just the hug first.

Because some things do not need words right away. Some things just need a body that says: I see you. I am here. You are safe.

Nova did not cry immediately. She held it together for about four seconds. And then something in her chest released and she let herself fall into her mother completely.

They stayed like that for a long moment.

"Talk to me," Reina said finally. Soft. No urgency. "What's going on?"

And Nova told her.

Not everything at first. Just the edges of it. The new girls in Simone's friend group. The comments about the rocking. The way Simone had gone quiet when they said it instead of saying something back. The way Nova had tried to hold herself still in the hallway and how exhausting that was and how she still could not stop and how she did not understand why something that was just part of her was apparently something to be fixed.

Reina listened to all of it without interrupting.

And when Nova finished Reina pulled back just enough to look at her daughter's face. Those honey brown eyes that caught the light like something precious. That face that had been lighting up rooms since before it had any idea it was doing it.

"Can I tell you something?" Reina said.

Nova nodded.

"This world would be so incredibly boring if we were all the same."

Nova blinked.

"Like genuinely," Reina continued, and there was a small smile pulling at the corner of her mouth now. "Can you imagine? Everybody sitting perfectly still. Nobody rocking or spinning or finding rocks in the woods or knowing every single fact about every anime character ever created." She tilted her head. "Actually that sounds terrible. I would not survive in that world."

Nova laughed. Just a small one. But it was real.

"Your uniqueness," Reina said, and her voice was softer now, more serious, "is not a flaw. It is not something to hide. It is not something to be embarrassed about. It is the thing that makes you Nova. And Nova —" she touched her daughter's face gently, " is the best thing I have ever had the privilege of knowing."

Nova looked at her mother for a long moment.

"But Simone "

"Simone is figuring out who she is," Reina said simply. "And sometimes when people are figuring out who they are they make choices that hurt the people they love. That does not make it okay. But it does not make it about you either."

She took Nova's hands in hers.

"Don't you ever let anyone make you feel any other way than exactly who you are. Don't you let anyone manipulate you into shrinking yourself so they can feel more comfortable. You hear me?"

Nova nodded slowly.

"Say it back to me."

Nova took a breath. "I won't let anyone make me feel any other way than who I am."

"Again."

"I won't let anyone make me feel any other way than who I am."

"One more time. Like you mean it."

Nova sat up a little straighter. Her locs fell back over her shoulders. Those honey brown eyes steadied.

"I will not let anyone make me feel any other way than who I am."

Reina smiled. The real one.

"There she is," she said quietly. "There is my Nova."

She Remembered — Reflection

- Have you ever started doing something differently, or stopped doing something you love, because of how someone looked at you? What did that feel like?
- What is the weight you are carrying right now that you have not told anyone about? What would it feel like to put it down?
- If your mom or grandmother or the woman who loves you most sat beside you right now and asked what's going on, what would you tell her?
- Say this out loud: I will not let anyone make me feel any other way than who I am. How did that feel?

> *A friendship that requires you to leave your sketchbook in your bag is not asking for your friendship. It is asking for your disappearance. And you, you are not a girl who disappears. You are a girl who shows up. Fully. As yourself. Every time.*

Remember Her

The weight she was carrying was not hers to carry alone. It never is. That is what the women who love us are for. Tell them. Let them sit beside you. Let them remind you who you are.

CHAPTER 4

The In-Between Girl

Nova had a theory about fitting in.

Her theory was that it was like learning a new language. Not impossible. Just, effortful. The kind of thing that took concentration and practice and a willingness to make mistakes and correct them quickly before anyone noticed. The kind of thing that felt unnatural at first but became more automatic the longer you did it.

She had been studying the language of Brianna and Kayla for weeks now.

She was getting better at it.

Not fluent. Not even close. But functional. Enough to get through a lunch period without saying the wrong thing or moving the wrong way or pulling out her sketchbook when sketchbooks were apparently not part of the approved vocabulary of their particular table.

The sketchbook stayed in her bag every day now.

She talked about the things they talked about. The shows Brianna liked. The drama that was apparently always happening somewhere in the sixth grade social ecosystem that Nova had not previously been paying attention to but was now learning to track. Who liked who. Who had said what to whom.

It was exhausting in a way she had not anticipated.

Not the information itself. Something else. Like the effort of tracking all of it was coming from a place inside her that was not designed for this particular kind of work.

But it was working.

Sort of.

Kayla had not said anything unkind to her in eleven days. Nova had counted.

Simone seemed, easier. More relaxed.

That was good.

She was fairly sure that was good.

The bows went first.

Not because anyone said anything. Nobody had to say anything. Nova was observant enough to understand that some things did not need to be said directly. Brianna wore her hair down or in a sleek ponytail. Kayla had two options, high bun or braids. Neither of them wore bows.

Nova looked at her reflection one Tuesday morning and saw the bows her mother had just put in, the gold star ones, her favorites, and something shifted in her chest.

She reached up.

"Leave them," Reina said from behind her. Not sharp. Just certain.

Nova's hands dropped.

She looked at her mother's reflection in the mirror. Reina was watching her with an expression that was careful and steady and carrying something underneath it that Nova could not quite read.

"They look beautiful," Reina said. "You look like you."

"I know," Nova said.

She left the bows in.

But she thought about them all day.

The morning ritual started to change in small ways she did not notice at first.

She still did it. She and her mother still stood at the mirror together and said the words the way they always had. But somewhere in the third week Nova realized she had been rushing through them.

Not skipping any, all the words were there, but moving through them at a pace that did not leave space for them to land.

I love myself I am more than enough today is going to be an amazing day I am intelligent I am strong I am powerful everything I need is already inside me I am a goddess I walk like I have ten thousand ancestors protecting me.

One breath. Done. Moving on.

Reina had not said anything about the rushing.

But one morning she put her hand gently on Nova's shoulder before Nova could turn away from the mirror and said again in a quiet voice. And they said it again. Slower. And the words landed differently the second time and Nova felt something in her chest that was close to tears without quite being tears.

She did not cry. She blinked it back and picked up her backpack and went downstairs for breakfast.

But her mother's hand on her shoulder stayed with her all day like something warm pressed against a cold place.

The moment that gave this chapter its name happened on a Friday.

It was the kind of Friday that felt like a reward for surviving the week, the last period of the day, the particular restless energy of a classroom full of kids who could feel the weekend just on the other side of the next forty-five minutes. Ms. Carter had given them free work time at the end of class and the room had that low pleasant hum of people doing their own things.

Nova had finished her work early. She sat at her desk with ten minutes left in the period and her hands folded on top of her notebook and absolutely nothing to do.

Her bag was on the hook beside her desk. The sketchbook was in the front pocket.

She looked at the bag.

She looked at the clock.

Ten minutes. Nobody was watching her.

Nova reached into her bag and pulled out the sketchbook.

She opened it to a fresh page.

She picked up her pencil.

And for ten minutes she drew. Not carefully. Not with one eye on the door. Just drew, her hand moving across the page in the way it always moved when she was not monitoring it, fast and instinctive and completely herself.

When the bell rang she looked down at what she had made.

It was good.

It was genuinely, undeniably good. The kind of good that happened when she stopped thinking about whether she should be drawing and just drew.

She sat there for a moment after the bell with the other students moving around her and she looked at this drawing that her hands had made in ten minutes of being allowed to be what they were and she felt something she had not felt in weeks.

Like herself.

Completely, simply, straightforwardly like herself.

And underneath that feeling was something else. Something harder. The recognition of what it had cost her to not feel this way. How much energy she had been spending carrying a version of herself that was carefully edited and monitored and adjusted.

You were born knowing exactly who you are.

Nana Rose's voice. Clear as if she were standing right there in the classroom.

Your only job is to remember.

Nova closed the sketchbook.

She put it back in her bag.

She stood up and put on her unicorn backpack and walked out of the classroom into the Friday afternoon hallway.

But something had shifted.

She could feel it in the way you feel a change in weather before it arrives. That something that had been building quietly in the background was about to require her full attention.

She did not know yet what she was going to do about it.

But she knew, with the deep certain knowing that lived in her bones rather than her brain, that she could not keep doing this.

That the in-between girl she had been trying to become was not a girl she wanted to be.

That Nova Cole, with her bows and her sketchbook and her stimming and her Glitter Force opinions and her rock collection and her Nutella sandwiches and her ten thousand ancestors, was not a problem to be solved.

She was a person to be known.

She Remembered — Reflection

◆ Have you ever caught yourself changing something about how you act or what you do to fit in with a group? What did you change?

◆ What happens to you when you spend a long time pretending to be someone you are not? How does your body feel? How does your spirit feel?

◆ What is your sketchbook, the thing that makes you feel most like yourself when you are doing it? How long has it been since you did it without anyone watching?

◆ What would you say to the in-between girl, the one who is trying to be someone else, if you could sit beside her right now?

> *You are not a problem to be solved. You are a person to be known. The right people will want to know all of you, not the edited version, not the carefully adjusted version, but the real complete full version. And if someone only wants the edited version, they do not want you. They want a performance. And you were born for more than performing.*

Remember Her

The in-between girl is not who you are. She is who you tried to become when you forgot that you were already enough. You are going to remember. You always do.

CHAPTER 5

The Moment of Truth

The winter showcase had been Ms. Carter's idea.

Every year the sixth grade held a showcase in the last week before winter break, a chance for students to share something they were proud of. A talent, a project, a piece of work. Something that was theirs. Ms. Carter had announced it in October and given them two months to prepare and Nova had known immediately, without hesitation, without deliberation, without a single moment of doubt, exactly what she was going to do.

She was going to show her manga.

Not just one drawing. A whole sequence, eight panels telling a short story about her character, the one with the finally-right eyes, the one she had been developing all semester. She had been working on it quietly, at home, in the safety of her pink room where nobody was watching and her hands could do what they did without anyone having opinions about it.

It was the best work she had ever done.

She knew that the way you knew things that were true about yourself, not from comparing it to anything else, just from the feeling it gave her when she looked at it.

The showcase was held in the school gymnasium on the Thursday before winter break.

Tables were set up around the perimeter of the room and students stood at their tables with their projects while families and other students moved through the space.

Nova's table was in the far left corner near the windows.

She had laid out her eight panels in sequence on the table, each one in a clear plastic sleeve, each one labeled in her neatest handwriting with the panel number and a short description of what was happening in the story. In the center she had placed a small card that said The Girl Who Remembered, A Manga Story by Nova Cole in letters she had spent forty-five minutes getting right.

She was proud of it.

Genuinely, straightforwardly, without any of the careful monitoring she had been doing for months, just proud. This was hers. All of it.

Simone came to find her twenty minutes into the showcase.

Nova saw her coming through the crowd and felt that familiar warmth that Simone's presence had given her since the first day of school.

But Simone was not alone.

Brianna and Kayla were with her. Both of them in their winter showcase best. They were talking to each other as they walked, Simone slightly between them, her gold purse catching the gymnasium light as she moved.

They stopped at Nova's table.

"Oh wow," Simone said, and she meant it. "Nova these are amazing. Look at this one" she pointed to panel five, the one Nova was most proud of. "The detail here is incredible."

"Thanks," Nova said.

Brianna leaned in and looked at the panels.

"These are really good," she said.

For a moment they all stood there together at Nova's table and it felt almost like the version of things Nova had imagined when the school year started. Four girls standing together. Looking at something one of them had made.

Almost.

"Hey," Kayla said, pulling out her phone. "Devon is over by the music setup. He said he might do a freestyle."

Brianna's head came up immediately. "Seriously?"

"He just texted." Kayla was already turning. "Come on before it gets crowded over there."

Brianna moved without hesitation.

They both looked at Simone.

Nova looked at Simone too.

It was a small moment. The kind that lasted maybe four seconds in real time. Kayla and Brianna already turning toward the other side of the gymnasium, the crowd between here and there, the thing they wanted to go see just beyond it.

And Simone standing at Nova's table.

Looking at her friends.

Looking at Nova.

Nova did not say anything. She would not ask. She would not make it a choice Simone had to navigate out loud because that was not fair and Nova knew it was not fair. These things were supposed to be easy. You were supposed to want to stay. If you had to be asked to stay the answer had already been given.

"I'll come find you after," Simone said.

And she went.

Nova watched her go.

And she felt it.

Not tears. Not anger. Something quieter than both of those things and somehow heavier. The particular weight of a moment where something you had been almost-knowing for a long time finally becomes completely known.

It was the same feeling her mother had described once. The feeling of realizing that the person you thought was standing with you had been somewhere else for a while. Not cruel. Not malicious. Just, somewhere else.

Nova had not fully understood it then.

She understood it now.

Her parents found her twenty minutes later still standing at her table.

Her mom took one look at her face and knew.

Not the details, she could not have known the details. But Reina Cole had been reading her daughter's face since before her daughter had words and she knew the difference between Nova's fine and Nova's fine.

She did not say anything in the gymnasium. She just stood beside Nova's table and looked at the panels with genuine attention and said you did this in a quiet voice that meant something more than the words.

"Yeah," Nova said.

"I am so proud of you."

Nova nodded.

Her dad put his arm around her shoulders. She let herself lean into him slightly.

In the car on the way home Simone texted.

Your panels were the best thing in the whole showcase. I'm serious. You're so talented Nova.

Nova read it twice.

She put her phone in her pocket.

She looked out the window at the dark streets passing by.

"Mom," she said.

"Yeah baby."

"Can we talk tonight?"

A pause. Short. The pause of someone shifting into something more present.

"Of course," Reina said. "We can talk about anything."

Nova nodded.

She looked back out the window.

She would find the words.

And her mother would listen to all of them.

She Remembered — Reflection

- Have you ever been in a moment where you realized someone you loved was not choosing you, not cruelly, just not choosing you? What did that feel like?
- What is the difference between a friend who stays because they want to and a friend who stays because you asked them to?
- Is there someone in your life you trust enough to say can we talk to when something gets all the way in? Who is that person for you?
- Nova stood at her table with her best work in front of her and felt the hurt of it, and she did not leave. She stayed. What does that tell you about who she is?

> *You are worth choosing. Not someday. Not when you make yourself easier to be around. Right now. As you are. The people who are meant for you will choose you, all of you, the manga and the stimming and the bows and everything. And the people who do not*

> *choose you, that is information. Not about your worth. About their capacity.*

Remember Her

Caring about someone and choosing them are two different things. Nova learned that on a Thursday night at a winter showcase. And the learning, even though it hurt, was the beginning of something better.

CHAPTER 6

The First Night I Chose Me

The house was quiet in the particular way it got quiet after a big evening.

Not empty quiet. Full quiet. The kind that settled over a home after everyone had come back from somewhere that mattered and the coats were hung and the shoes were off and the ordinary warmth of being inside your own space wrapped around you like something you had not realized you needed until you felt it.

Nova sat on her bed.

She had changed out of her showcase outfit and was in her pajamas now with her locs loose around her shoulders the way she wore them at home when nobody was watching. Her sketchbook was on the desk. She had not opened it.

She was looking at the wall.

Not at anything specific on the wall. Just, at the wall. The familiar pink of it. The small framed print her mother had hung there when they first moved in that said you are exactly where you are supposed to be in gold letters on a white background. Nova had read those words approximately ten thousand times. Tonight they landed differently than they usually did.

She heard her mother's footsteps in the hallway.

The particular rhythm of them, not hurried, not hesitant, just steady and purposeful, told Nova everything before the knock came.

"Come in," she said.

Reina opened the door and looked at her daughter.

This was the thing about her mother that Nova had never quite been able to put into words but had always felt, the way Reina looked at her. Not at the surface of her. At her. The actual her underneath all of that.

Tonight the instrument was telling her something.

Nova could see it in the slight shift around her mother's eyes. The way she did not ask are you okay, because Reina Cole never asked questions she already knew the answer to, but simply crossed the room and sat down on the bed beside her daughter.

Close. Not touching yet. Just present.

They sat like that for a moment.

And then Reina opened her arms.

Nova went into them without thinking about it. Her body simply moved the way it moved when it found the place it was safest, completely and without reservation. She tucked herself against her mother's side and felt the familiar weight of Reina's arms around her and something in her chest that had been held carefully in place all evening began, slowly, carefully, to release.

She did not cry immediately.

She held it for about four seconds.

And then she did not hold it anymore.

It was not the dramatic kind of crying. Not gasping or shaking. Just the quiet steady kind that came from somewhere deep and real.

Reina held her and did not say anything. Did not try to fix it or reframe it or rush to the part where everything was okay. She just held her daughter and let her cry.

When the crying settled Reina's hand moved slowly over Nova's locs. The way she had done since Nova was small. The gesture that meant I'm here, I've got you, take all the time you need.

"Talk to me," she said finally. "What's going on?"

Nova told her.

Not in a perfect linear narrative. In the way things actually came out when you were twelve and tired and had been carrying something for longer than you should have, in pieces. Out of order. The showcase first and then further back to the hallway and Kayla and the stutter and the word weird and the sketchbook that had stayed in the bag and the bows she had almost taken out and the morning ritual she had been rushing through.

Reina listened to all of it.

When Nova finished Reina was quiet for a moment.

Then she said: “Can I tell you something?”

Nova nodded against her mother’s shoulder.

“I know how that feels.”

Nova lifted her head slightly.

“Not the exact same situation,” Reina said. “But the feeling. That particular feeling of being in a room with people and realizing that the person you thought was standing with you has been somewhere else for a while.” She paused. “I know that feeling. And I want you to know, it is one of the hardest feelings there is. And you are allowed to feel it completely.”

“It hurts,” Nova said simply.

“I know it does baby.”

They sat with that for a moment. Not rushing past it.

“Can I ask you something?” Reina said eventually.

“Yeah.”

“The sketchbook. The bows. The morning ritual you’ve been rushing through.” She felt Nova go slightly still. “Did you think I didn’t notice?”

Nova did not answer right away.

“I was hoping you didn’t,” she said finally.

Reina made a sound that was not quite a laugh but was adjacent to one. Warm and wry and full of something that knew its daughter very well.

"Nova Renee Cole," she said. "I have been watching you since before you could hold your own head up. There is nothing you do that I do not notice."

"That's a lot of pressure," Nova said.

"It is," Reina agreed. "I'm sorry about that." She pulled back just enough to look at her daughter's face. "I want to ask you something and I want you to answer it honestly. Not the answer you think I want. The real one."

Nova nodded.

"When you left the sketchbook in your bag, when you held your stim in the hallway, when you rushed through our ritual in the morning, did it feel like you? Did any of it feel like Nova?"

The question sat in the room between them.

Nova looked at her mother.

"No," she said.

"No," Reina repeated quietly.

"It felt like I was wearing something that didn't fit," Nova said. "Like a costume. That looked right from the outside maybe but from the inside felt wrong and I kept thinking maybe I just needed to get used to it. But it never did."

Reina looked at her daughter for a long moment.

"Okay," she said. "I want you to hear me say something and I want you to really let it in. Not just hear it. Let it in." She took Nova's hands in hers. "A friendship that requires you to leave your sketchbook in your bag is not asking for your friendship. It is asking for your disappearance. And you" her voice was steady and certain and full of something that had been earned through hard experience, "— are not a girl who disappears. Do you hear me?"

Nova felt the words land. All the way in.

"Do you hear me?" Reina asked again. Softer.

"Yeah," Nova said. "I hear you."

"Say it back."

Nova blinked. "What?"

"What I just said. Say it back to me."

Nova looked at her mother. At the steadiness in her face. At the complete absence of doubt in her eyes about Nova herself. About who she was and what she deserved.

"A friendship that requires me to leave my sketchbook in my bag," Nova began slowly, finding each word, "is not asking for my friendship. It's asking for my disappearance."

"And you are"

"And I am not a girl who disappears."

"Again."

"I am not a girl who disappears."

"One more time. Like you mean every word."

Nova took a breath.

She thought about her character. The one with the finally-right eyes. The Girl Who Remembered.

She thought about Nana Rose in her yellow dress saying you were born knowing exactly who you are.

"I am not a girl who disappears," she said. And meant every single word.

Reina smiled. The real one.

"There she is," she said softly. "There is my Nova."

Before her mother left for the night Nova opened her sketchbook.

She turned to a fresh page.

She picked up her pencil.

And she drew without monitoring it. Without one eye on the door. Without the careful adjusted version of herself sitting between her hand and the page.

Just Nova. Pencil. Paper.

The drawing that emerged was simple. A girl sitting on a bed. Locs loose around her shoulders. A mug in her hands. A small framed print on the wall behind her.

The girl in the drawing was smiling.

Not a performed smile. Not the smile of someone who was doing the job of being okay.

Just a girl who had put something heavy down and was feeling, for the first time in a long time, the particular lightness of that.

Nova looked at the drawing.

She looked at it for a long time.

Then she wrote three words at the bottom of the page in her neatest handwriting.

She remembered herself.

She closed the sketchbook.

She turned off her light.

And Nova Cole, with her locs and her honey brown eyes and her ten thousand ancestors and her manga and her rock collection and her Nutella sandwiches and her stimming and her stutter and every single thing that made her completely and entirely herself, went to sleep.

She Remembered — Reflection

◆ Is there someone in your life you trust enough to tell the whole truth to, not the edited version, not the version that makes you seem okay, but the real one? When was the last time you told them?

◆ What is the thing you stopped doing, or started hiding, to fit in somewhere? What would it feel like to do it freely again?

◆ What would you write at the bottom of your own drawing tonight? What three words describe where you are right now?

◆ Say it out loud: I am not a girl who disappears. How did that feel in your body?

> *You did not fix everything tonight. The friendship is still complicated. Middle school is still middle school. But something shifted. Because you told the truth, to your mother and then to yourself, and the truth has a way of making space for things to change. You are not a girl who disappears. Say that every morning until it lives in your bones.*

Remember Her

She remembered herself. Three words. Written at the bottom of a drawing. By a twelve year old girl who had just put something heavy down. That is the whole story. That is everything.

CHAPTER 7

My Voice Is Mine

The first day back after winter break had a particular feeling that Nova had always liked.

Not the Sunday night dread that sometimes preceded the first day of a new school week. Something cleaner than that. The feeling of a fresh page, all the mistakes and adjustments and careful monitoring of the previous semester on one side of a clear line and everything that came next on the other.

Nova stood in front of her mirror on the first Monday of January and looked at herself.

Pink dress. Not the same one as the first day, a new one, deep rose with buttons down the front that her grandmother had given her for Christmas. Two bows. The gold star ones. Her locs falling in two perfect sections over her shoulders. Tortoiseshell glasses. Her unicorn backpack by the door throwing its small rainbows across the wall.

She looked like herself.

Completely. Without adjustment.

They said the words together. The whole ritual. Every line. Slowly. With the spaces between them that allowed each one to land properly before the next arrived.

I love myself.

I am more than enough.

Today is going to be an amazing day.

I am intelligent. I am strong. I am powerful.

Everything I need is already inside me.

I am a goddess.

I walk like I have ten thousand ancestors protecting me.

They looked at each other in the mirror. Reina's hands squeezed Nova's shoulders gently.

"There she is," her mother said softly.

"There I am," Nova said.

And meant it.

She carried her sketchbook in her hand when she walked into school.

Not in her bag. Not tucked away in the front pocket. In her hand. Visible. Hers.

It was a small thing. It was also not a small thing at all.

She walked down the main hallway past the mural, YOU BELONG HERE and felt it the way she had felt it on the very first day. Not as a reassurance she needed. As a fact she already knew.

She belonged here.

This version. The real one.

Simone came in four minutes before the bell.

She saw Nova immediately. She walked over and slid into the seat beside Nova and for a moment they just looked at each other the way you looked at someone after a gap of time, checking, recalibrating, finding the frequency again.

"Hey," Simone said.

"Hey," Nova said.

"How was your break?"

"Good. Really good actually." Nova paused. "I finished the manga sequence. Added three more panels."

Simone's face opened. "Can I see?"

Nova opened her sketchbook to the new panels and slid it across the desk.

Simone looked at them for a long moment. Really looked.

"Nova," she said. "This one." She pointed to the second new panel, the one where the character finally turned fully toward her own reflection and looked at it without flinching. "This one is my favorite thing you've ever drawn."

Nova looked at the panel.

"Thanks," Nova said.

"I mean it." Simone slid the sketchbook back. She was quiet for a moment. And then, in the particular way that Simone said true things when she had decided to say them, "I'm sorry. About the showcase. I should have stayed."

Nova looked at her.

"You don't have to"

"I know I don't have to," Simone said. "I want to. Because it wasn't right and I knew it wasn't right when I did it and I did it anyway." She stopped. Looked at her hands. "I'm still figuring out how to be in two places at once. I'm not very good at it."

Nova was quiet for a moment.

"I know," she said finally. "I'm not mad at you."

"You were though. A little."

"A little," Nova admitted. "But I'm not anymore."

Simone looked at her. "How come?"

"Because I figured something out over break," she said. "And it kind of made everything else feel smaller."

"What did you figure out?"

Nova picked up her sketchbook. Held it. The familiar weight of it in her hand.

"That this is mine," she said simply. "My drawing. My stimming. My bows. My way of talking. All of it. It's mine. And I spent a whole semester trying to put it away so other people would be more comfortable and all it did was make me uncomfortable. She paused. "So I decided I'm not doing that anymore."

Simone looked at her for a long moment.

"Just like that?" she said.

"Just like that."

"That's" Simone seemed to be searching for the right word. "That's kind of brave."

"My nana says it's not brave," Nova said. "She says being yourself is just the most efficient option. Everything else takes too much energy."

Simone laughed. The real laugh. The one that started in her chest.

"I like your nana," she said.

"Everyone likes my nana," Nova said. "It's basically her superpower."

The bell rang.

The first real test came at lunch.

Nova carried her sketchbook to the cafeteria the way she had carried it in her hand all morning, visibly, without apology. She got her lunch and found the table and sat down and opened it before Brianna and Kayla even arrived.

Brianna arrived first. She looked at the open sketchbook. She looked at Nova.

"You're drawing again," she said.

"I never stopped," Nova said. "I just started doing it everywhere again."

Brianna sat down. She leaned slightly toward the sketchbook, that genuine curiosity she always had about Nova's work showing up automatically.

"What is this one?"

"New character," Nova said. "She's a healer. She can absorb other people's pain but she has to be careful not to absorb too much or she loses herself."

Brianna looked at the half-finished drawing. "That's deep for a character."

"All the best characters are," Nova said.

Kayla arrived and sat down and said nothing. Not unkindly. Just nothing.

Nova let the nothing be nothing and kept drawing.

Simone slid into the seat across from her and immediately started asking questions about the healer character and Nova answered all of them with the focused enthusiasm she brought to things she actually cared about.

Under the table her foot tapped.

Her hand moved across the page.

She ate her Nutella sandwich in between answers.

It was not perfect. The social ecosystem of their lunch table was not suddenly simple.

But Nova was herself in it.

Completely. Without apology.

And that, that particular feeling of being entirely present in her own life, was worth more than smooth.

After school Ms. Carter stopped her on the way out.

“Nova.” She held out a folded piece of paper. “I wanted to give you this before you left.”

Nova took it. Unfolded it.

It was a printout of a call for submissions for a regional middle school art showcase, a competition open to students across the district. The deadline was in March. The category listed first was sequential art and illustration.

Manga.

“I think you should enter,” Ms. Carter said. “The panels you showed at the winter showcase were exceptional. I mean that.”

Nova looked at the paper. At the deadline. At the category.

“You really think so?”

“I really think so,” Ms. Carter said. “I think you have a specific gift Nova. The kind that deserves to be seen beyond this building.” She paused. “But more than that, I think you know you have it. And I think part of growing up is learning to let yourself be seen in proportion to what you actually are.”

Nova folded the paper carefully.

“Thank you Ms. Carter.”

“Don’t thank me,” Ms. Carter said. “Enter.”

Nova put the paper in her sketchbook, between two pages, safe, and walked out of school into the January afternoon.

Her dad’s car was in the pickup line.

She slid into the back seat.

“Good day?” he asked.

Nova thought about Simone’s apology and Brianna leaning toward her drawing and her foot tapping freely under the table and Ms. Carter’s folded paper and the way she had said the morning words this morning and meant every single one.

“Yeah,” she said. “Really good.”

Her dad looked at her in the rearview mirror.

“You seem like yourself,” he said.

Nova looked out the window at the January sky.

“I am,” she said simply.

And she was.

She Remembered — Reflection

- What would it look like for you to carry your sketchbook, whatever your sketchbook is, visibly and without apology tomorrow?
- Is there someone in your life who has apologized to you in a way that felt real? How did you receive it?
- What is the thing that is specifically yours, your gift, your way of seeing, your particular kind of brilliant, that deserves to be seen beyond the room you are currently in?
- What does it feel like to be entirely present in your own life? Can you think of a moment when you felt that way?

> *My voice is mine. My gifts are mine. My way of moving through the world is mine. I do not need anyone’s permission to be fully present in my own life. I show up as myself today and every day. Completely. Without apology.*

Remember Her

Part of growing up is learning to let yourself be seen in proportion to what you actually are. Ms. Carter said that. Write it down. Say it to your mirror. Let it become the thing you believe about yourself. Because it is already true.

CHAPTER 8

She Always Had It

The regional art showcase application sat on Nova's desk for three days before she filled it out.

Not because she was uncertain about whether she wanted to enter. She was certain. Ms. Carter's words had landed in her the way true things landed, cleanly, without resistance, finding the place they were meant to go and staying there.

Part of growing up is learning to let yourself be seen in proportion to what you actually are.

She was certain.

She was just, taking her time with it. The way she took her time with things that mattered. Sitting with the weight of them. Letting the reality of what she was about to do settle into her body before she committed to it.

Because this was different from the winter showcase.

The winter showcase had been inside her school. Teachers and parents and students who already knew her.

The regional showcase was different. Nobody there would know her. They would see the work first. Just the work.

She picked up her pen on the fourth day.

She filled out the application.

She put it in her backpack to give to Ms. Carter in the morning.

And then she opened her sketchbook and worked on the sequence for two hours because the application was done and there was nothing left to do but make the work as good as it could possibly be.

She told Simone the next day at lunch.

Just Simone, not at the full table, but in the five minutes before Brianna and Kayla arrived when it was just the two of them.

"I entered the regional showcase," Nova said.

Simone put down her fork. "Nova."

"Ms. Carter told me about it."

"Nova." Simone said her name again like it was doing a different job the second time. Like it meant do you understand what this is and I am so proud of you and of course you did all at once.

"I know," Nova said.

"Can I see the full sequence? All of it?"

Nova opened her sketchbook to the beginning of The Girl Who Remembered and slid it across the table.

Simone read it the way you read something that has been made well, slowly, with her full attention, panel by panel, not rushing toward the ending.

When she reached the final panel she sat with it for a long moment before looking up.

"This is about you," she said.

Nova had not said that to anyone. Not planned to say it. It was just true and Simone had seen it and there was no point in pretending otherwise.

"Yeah," she said.

"It's about this year," Simone said. "The whole semester. You kind of, drew your way through it."

"I always draw my way through things."

"I know." Simone slid the sketchbook back. Her voice was quiet. "I'm sorry I made it harder."

"Simone"

"I am though." She looked directly at Nova. "I saw what was happening. With Kayla and how she talked to you sometimes. And I didn't say anything."

Nova looked at her best friend.

"You can't keep everybody happy," she said.

"You can't," Simone agreed. "I'm working on it. Figuring out when to say something."

"Me too," Nova said.

They looked at each other. The particular look of two people who had been through something together and were coming out the other side with a better understanding of each other than they had going in.

"We're both figuring it out," Simone said.

"Yeah," Nova said. "I think that's just what this age is."

The weeks between January and March had a quality Nova had not experienced much before.

Purposeful. That was the word. She had always been a purposeful person in small ways, purposeful about her drawings, purposeful about her rock collection, purposeful about the morning ritual. But this was something larger. A purpose that organized the other purposes around it. A center.

She worked on the sequence every day. Not all day, she still did her schoolwork and her reading and her science experiments and her walks in the woods with her dad when the weather allowed. But every day there was time specifically for The Girl Who Remembered. Time that was protected. Time that was hers.

Reina noticed the shift. She did not make a big deal of it, that was not her way, but Nova caught her watching sometimes with an expression that was quiet and certain and full of something that had been earned through paying attention.

One evening Nova looked up from her sketchbook to find her mother in the doorway of her room with that expression.

"What?" Nova said.

"Nothing," Reina said. "Just looking at you."

"Why?"

Reina smiled. The real one. "Because you look like yourself."

Nova looked down at her drawing. The girl on the page with the finally-right eyes looking directly out at whoever was looking.

"I feel like myself," she said.

"I know," her mother said. "It shows."

The night before the showcase Nova sat at her desk and looked at the complete sequence.

Eleven panels now. The original eight plus three she had added.

She had been thinking about the ending since September without knowing she was thinking about it. The character's journey had been unclear to her for most of the semester, she knew the beginning, knew the middle, but the ending had stayed just out of reach.

And then one morning in February she had woken up and known.

The ending was not the girl being saved. It was not the girl winning something or defeating someone or having a dramatic moment of transformation. It was simpler than that and harder than that and more true than either of those things.

The ending was the girl looking in the mirror.

Just that. Just a girl standing in front of her own reflection. Looking at herself, really looking. And in the reflection a small smile. Not performed. Not for anyone watching. Just the quiet private smile of someone who had come back from somewhere and was glad to be home.

Below the final panel Nova had written three words in her neatest lettering.

She remembered herself.

She looked at those words now in the quiet of her bedroom.

She thought about everything the year had held. The first day with her sparkly backpack throwing rainbows down the hallway. Simone walking over like it was the obvious thing to do. The mural. You belong here. The hallway with Kayla and the word weird landing in her chest like something cold. The sketchbook in the bag. The bows she had almost taken out. The rushed mornings.

And then the other side of it. The conversation with her mother. The three words at the bottom of the drawing. Winter break and Nana Rose's stories and the January morning when she had walked back into school carrying her sketchbook in her hand.

The healer character. Ms. Carter's folded paper. Simone's real laugh. Her foot tapping freely under the lunch table.

All of it had been the story.

Not just the story in the sketchbook. Her story. Nova Cole's sixth grade story. The year she had almost forgotten herself and then remembered.

She closed the sketchbook gently.

She went to her mirror.

She looked at herself. Just herself. No performance. No monitoring. Just Nova.

"I always had it," she said quietly to her reflection.

Not as a question. Not as something she was trying to convince herself of.

As a fact.

She had always had it. The gift and the knowing and the particular way her brain worked and the eyes that saw everything and the hands that could make what she saw into something real on a page. All of it had always been there. Through the sketchbook in the bag and the bows she almost took out and the months of careful adjusting.

It had been there the whole time.

Waiting.

The way it always waited.

The way she always waited for herself.

"There she is," she said softly.

And smiled the real smile.

She Remembered — Reflection

- What is the thing you have always been able to do, naturally, without being taught, from as far back as you can remember, that you sometimes forget to count as a gift?
- Is there a story you have been living this year that you have not yet put into words? What would you call it if it were a book?
- What would you write at the bottom of your own drawing? What three words describe your story this year?
- What would it feel like to look in the mirror tonight and say: I always had it, and mean it?

> *You have always had it. Everything you need. Everything you are. It was never lost. You were just looking for it in the wrong places. It was here. It has always been here. Right here inside you where it has always lived. The gift does not come from the good days. It comes from you. It is you.*

Remember Her

She always had it. The power was never gone. It was waiting, patiently, faithfully, with more grace than she had given herself, for her to come back and claim it. You have the same power waiting for you. Go claim it.

CHAPTER 9

Whole Not Half

The regional showcase was held on a Saturday morning in March at a school across town that was bigger than Nova's.

Nova's whole family came.

Her parents, both of them, her dad in his good jacket, her mom in the deep gold dress that Nova had always loved because it made her look like exactly who she was. Nana Rose, who had driven three hours again, because Nana Rose did not miss things that mattered, in her yellow dress. Nova had never been sure if it was the same yellow dress or a different one that was identical to the first one. It did not matter. What mattered was the yellow and what the yellow meant which was I am here and I see you and you are loved.

Simone came too.

She had asked, quietly, just the two of them, if she could. And Nova had said yes without hesitating because she meant it without hesitating.

Nova's table was in the east section of the gymnasium.

She set up her panels with the same care she had used at the winter showcase, each one in its clear plastic sleeve, each one labeled, the title card in the center. The Girl Who Remembered, A Manga Story by Nova Cole.

Eleven panels this time instead of eight.

A complete story.

Nana Rose stood beside her while she set up and did not say anything for a long moment. Just looked at the panels in sequence, slowly, fully, panel by panel.

When she reached the final one she was quiet for a long time.

"Nova girl," she said finally.

"Yeah?"

"Do you know what you made here?"

Nova looked at her sequence. At the girl with the finally-right eyes. At the whole story told in eleven panels, the forgetting and the carrying and the moment of clarity and the conversation and the choosing and the returning. At the three words at the bottom of the last panel.

"I think so," she said.

"You made your story," Nana Rose said. "You took what this year gave you and you turned it into something that is going to make other girls feel less alone." She looked at her granddaughter with those sharp warm eyes that missed nothing. "That is a gift. Not just the drawing. The willingness to be honest enough to make something true."

Nova felt the words land the way Nana Rose's words always landed, all the way in, past the surface, finding the place they were meant to go.

"You told me," Nova said. "At the beginning of the year. You told me my only job was to remember."

"I did," Nana Rose said.

"I forgot for a while."

"I know."

"But I remembered."

Nana Rose smiled. The full warm certain smile of a woman who had been watching the people she loved find their way back to themselves for decades and had never once stopped believing they would.

"You always do," she said. "That is who you come from."

The judges came through at eleven.

Three of them, adults with lanyards and clipboards who moved through the space with the focused attention of people who knew what they were looking for. Nova watched them approach her table from across the room and felt her foot start its steady tap against the gymnasium floor.

They stopped at her panels.

One of them, a woman with natural hair and reading glasses and the kind of stillness that meant she was thinking rather than waiting, looked at the sequence for a long time. Panel by panel. Beginning to end. Then she went back to the beginning and looked again.

Nova stood at her table and did not fidget. Did not rush to explain. Did not perform composure. Just stood there, foot tapping, hands finding their small pattern at her sides, and let the work speak for itself.

Because it could.

She knew it could.

The woman looked up.

“Did you write the story too?” she asked. “Or just illustrate it?”

“Both,” Nova said. “It’s my story. I wrote it and drew it.”

The woman looked at her for a moment with an expression that was assessing but not unkind.

“How old are you?”

“Twelve.”

A pause. Not a long one.

“This is exceptional work,” the woman said. Not as flattery. As information. “The visual storytelling in panel five specifically, the way the light changes across these three frames, that is a technique that students much older than you struggle to execute.” She looked back at the sequence. “You have a real gift.”

“Thank you,” Nova said.

She meant it completely.

She did not deflect it or minimize it or look at the floor while she said it. She received it the way her mother had taught her to receive true things, directly, with her full self present, without apology.

The judges moved on.

She did not win first place.

She won second.

The first place ribbon went to an eighth grader who had made an enormous oil painting that was technically extraordinary and visually stunning and deserved every bit of the recognition it received. Nova looked at it when the awards were announced and felt genuine admiration for it, the clean uncomplicated admiration of someone who respected craft and could recognize it without needing to diminish it to make space for her own.

Her second place ribbon was deep blue with gold lettering.

She held it in both hands and looked at it.

"Second place at a regional showcase," her dad said from beside her. "In sixth grade."

"Yeah," Nova said.

"Nova."

"I know Dad."

"Do you though?" He put his hand on her shoulder. "Do you actually know what that means?"

Nova looked at the ribbon. At the gold lettering. At the gymnasium full of students and families and art made by kids who cared about making things.

She thought about everything the year had held.

"Yeah," Nova said quietly. "I actually know."

On the drive home Nana Rose sat in the back seat with Nova and held her hand the way she had held her hand since Nova was small enough to fit entirely in her lap.

They did not talk much. The day had been full enough that silence felt right.

At some point Nana Rose said: "You know what the ribbon means?"

"Second place," Nova said.

"No," Nana Rose said. "It means someone saw you. Someone who did not know you walked past your work and saw you in it and said, this one. This one deserves to be recognized." She squeezed Nova's hand. "That is what the ribbon means. Not a number. Recognition. Someone seeing what you made and knowing it came from something real."

Nova looked at the ribbon in her lap.

"You were born knowing exactly who you are," Nana Rose said. One more time. "The world tried to make you forget."

"It did," Nova said.

"But you remembered."

Nova looked out the window at the March afternoon passing by. The trees coming back to themselves after winter.

"I remembered," she said.

Nana Rose squeezed her hand once more.

And did not say anything else.

Because there was nothing else to say.

She Remembered — Reflection

◆ Have you ever received a compliment or recognition for something you worked hard on and deflected it instead of receiving it? Why do you think you did that?

◆ What does it feel like to be seen, really seen, by someone who did not know you before they saw your work? Why does that feel different from being seen by people who already love you?

◆ Who is your Nana Rose, the person in your life who holds your hand without needing to say much? Have you told them what they mean to you?

◆ What would it mean to receive your own gifts fully, to know what you have without minimizing it, without deflecting, without shrinking from the truth of it?

> *You are whole. Not a half waiting to be completed. Not a work in progress waiting to be finished. Whole. Right now. As you are. The ribbon was not what made Nova whole. She was already whole. The ribbon was just the world catching up to what she already knew about herself. You are whole right now. In this moment. Exactly as you are.*

Remember Her

Someone seeing what you made and knowing it came from something real, that is the whole point. Not the prize. The recognition of something true. That is what you are building toward. Not accolades. A life full of work that comes from something real. Keep building.

CHAPTER 10

She Remembered

The last day of sixth grade arrived the way last days always did, faster than expected and slower than it felt like it should have been, both things true at the same time.

Nova sat at her desk in Ms. Carter's homeroom on the last morning of the school year and looked around the room with the particular attention she gave things she wanted to remember accurately. Not nostalgically. But accurately. This room. These people. This specific chapter of her life that was ending today and would not come back in exactly this form.

She wanted to see it clearly before it was over.

Brianna was across the room talking to someone Nova did not know well, her end-of-year energy brighter than her usual careful composure. She caught Nova's eye at one point and did something small with her expression. Not a full smile. Just an acknowledgment. A nod between two people who had been in the same space for a year and had arrived at a version of mutual respect that neither of them had expected in September.

Nova nodded back.

Kayla was beside Brianna, already talking about summer plans. She had not said anything unkind to Nova since before winter break. Nova did not know if that was a permanent change or a temporary one and she had decided she did not need to know. What she knew was that she had not adjusted herself for Kayla in months. Had not held her stim or left her sketchbook in her bag or rushed her morning ritual because of anything Kayla said or did.

That was enough to know.

Simone slid into the seat beside her.

They looked at each other.

A whole school year in that look. Everything it had held, the anime conversations and the good lunches and the winter showcase and the January morning and all the complicated territory in between. The friendship that had been tested and bent and had not broken because both of them, imperfectly, gradually, with more stumbling than either of them would have preferred, had found their way back to choosing each other.

"Last day," Simone said.

"Last day," Nova agreed.

"How are you feeling?"

Nova thought about it. The real answer.

"Like I actually finished something," she said. "Not just the school year. Something bigger than that."

Simone nodded slowly. "Yeah," she said. "Me too."

Ms. Carter did something at the end of homeroom that Nova had not expected.

She gave each student a small card. Not a report card or an award or anything official. Just a small card, white with a simple border, and on each one she had written something specific to that student. Not a grade. Something she had observed. Something true.

Nova turned her card over.

In Ms. Carter's neat handwriting it said:

Nova, You came in knowing who you were. You spent some time forgetting. And then you remembered. Watching that happen was one of the best things about this year. Keep making true things. The world needs them., Ms. Carter

Nova read it twice.

She folded it carefully and put it in her sketchbook between two pages.

Safe. Where the important things went.

She looked up and found Ms. Carter looking at her from across the room with that expression, the one that had been present since the very first day, the one that said I see you and what I see is worth seeing.

Nova mouthed thank you.

Ms. Carter nodded once. Simple. Certain.

The bell rang.

Her dad picked her up after the final bell.

She slid into the back seat with her backpack and her sketchbook and her second-place ribbon that she had been carrying in the front pocket of her bag since March.

“Last day,” her dad said.

“Last day.”

“How was it?”

Nova looked out the window as the school building slid past for the last time this year. The mural visible through the front windows, YOU BELONG HERE, catching the June afternoon light.

“It was good,” she said. “Really good. But also” she paused, finding the words. “Also a lot. The whole year was a lot.”

“Yeah,” her dad said. “Sixth grade usually is.”

“Did you have a year like this?” Nova asked. “Where you kind of lost yourself for a while and then found your way back?”

Her dad was quiet for a moment. The quiet of someone actually considering the question rather than reaching for the nearest reassuring answer.

"Yeah," he said. "I did. Different circumstances. Same feeling."

"What helped?"

"Time," he said. "And someone who saw me clearly. And deciding that who I actually was mattered more than who was convenient to be."

Nova thought about that.

"That's good advice," she said.

"I had good people around me," he said. "Same as you."

Nova looked out the window at the familiar streets of her neighborhood passing by. The trees in full summer green now, the pale promise of March fulfilled, the branches thick and certain with what they had become.

She thought about the year.

About all of it.

Not just the hard parts, though the hard parts had been real and she was not going to pretend otherwise. But all of it. The first day and the mural and Simone walking over like it was the obvious thing to do. The sketchbook on the desk in Ms. Carter's class. The showcase and the ribbon and Nana Rose's hand in hers on the drive home. The morning ritual said slowly. The morning ritual meant.

She thought about the girl in the final panel of her sequence. The one with the finally-right eyes looking directly out at whoever was looking. The real smile at the bottom.

She remembered herself.

That girl was her.

Had always been her.

Would always be her, no matter what sixth grade threw at her, no matter what seventh grade was going to bring, no matter what the world decided to say about her stimming or her stutter or her sketchbook or her bows or any of the thousand specific things that made her completely and entirely Nova Cole.

She was the girl who remembered.

And she was never going to forget again.

That night she sat at her desk and opened her sketchbook to a fresh page.

She picked up her pencil.

She thought about the new character. The one who kept showing up at the edges of her imagination. The one whose story she did not know yet.

She started to draw.

The character emerged from the page the way characters always did when Nova stopped thinking about them and just let her hands do what they knew how to do. The face first. Then the shoulders. Then the hands. Strong hands. The hands of someone who made things.

Nova looked at what she had so far.

The character looked back.

"What's your story?" Nova asked her quietly.

The character did not answer. Of course she did not answer. She was a drawing. She existed in the space between what Nova knew and what Nova had not yet discovered.

Nova smiled.

She kept drawing.

Her foot tapped against the floor.

Her locs fell forward over her shoulders.

The pink room held her.

And outside her window the June evening settled into the neighborhood like something warm and certain, the long light of a day that had been lived fully and was not yet ready to be done.

Nova Cole.

Twelve years old.

Artist. Creator. Collector of rocks and truths and things worth remembering.

A girl who had forgotten herself once and found her way back.

A girl who carried ten thousand ancestors in her bones.

A girl who walked into every room like she belonged there.

Because she did.

She always had.

She always would.

She Remembered — Reflection

◆ What is the most important thing you learned about yourself this year? Not from a test. From your life.

◆ What is the new story you are about to start, the next chapter, the next school year, the next version of your life, and what do you want to carry into it?

◆ What would you write on your own card the way Ms. Carter wrote on Nova's? What is the truest thing about you that deserves to be written down and kept safe?

◆ Say the whole morning ritual out loud right now. Every word. Slowly. Meaning all of it.

> *You came in knowing who you were. You may have spent some time forgetting. And now you are remembering. That is the whole story. That is always the whole story. The forgetting is not failure. It is human. And the remembering, the coming back, the choosing yourself again, the saying the words in the mirror and meaning them, that is the work of a lifetime. Keep doing it. She is worth it.*

Remember Her

She remembered. And when she remembered, she was her. And she was never going to forget again. Neither are you.

A NOTE FROM THE AUTHOR

Nova remembered herself at twelve.

She will forget again sometimes. That is part of being human. The world is loud and the social dynamics of middle school are real and the pressure to shrink yourself to fit into spaces that were not designed for your specific kind of wonderful is something that does not go away after one good semester.

But she knows the way back now.

She will always know the way back.

The morning ritual. The sketchbook in her hand. The mirror and the words. The women who love her. The circle that holds her.

I wrote this book for my daughter. The girl who came into this world fighting before she ever took her first breath. The girl who wakes up every morning with more joy than most people carry in a week. The girl who is unapologetic about who she is in every space she enters and has taught me more about remembering myself than anything else ever has.

Nova is for her.

And Nova is for you.

For the girl who is just beginning. For the girl who is in the middle of forgetting. For the girl who is finding her way back. For the girl who has never forgotten and needs to see herself in a story so she knows how to stay.

You were born knowing exactly who you are.

The world is going to try to make you forget.

Your only job is to remember.

With love,

Kendra Tamika

This section is for you.

Nova kept a journal all year. She drew in it and wrote in it and said the things she could not yet say out loud. This is your space to do the same thing. There are no wrong answers here. There is only your truth. Write it down. Come back to it. Let it show you who you are.

Journal Prompt 1

Who are you when nobody is watching? Describe yourself, not how others see you, not the version you perform. The real version. The one who exists in your room when the door is closed.

Journal Prompt 2

What is your sketchbook? What is the thing you do that makes you feel most completely like yourself? When did you last do it without anyone watching?

Journal Prompt 3

Is there something about yourself that you have been hiding or minimizing to fit in somewhere? What would it feel like to bring it fully into the light?

Journal Prompt 4

Write your morning ritual. The words you want to say to yourself every morning before the day begins. Make them yours. Make them true.

Journal Prompt 5

Write a letter to the girl you were at the beginning of this year. What do you want to tell her? What does she need to know?

Journal Prompt 6

Who is the Nova in your life, the girl you most want to be like, who moves through the world exactly as herself without apology? What is it about her that you admire?

Journal Prompt 7

What is the thing you want to create, build, make, or become in the next year? Write it in the present tense as if it is already true.

Journal Prompt 8

Write the three words that describe who you are at your most fully yourself. Carry them with you.

Journal Prompt 9

Who are the people in your life who make you feel most like yourself? What do they do that makes you feel that way?

Journal Prompt 10

Finish this sentence with everything you have: I remember her. She is...

ACKNOWLEDGEMENTS

This book would not exist without the people who held me and the people who inspired me.

To my daughter, you are Nova. You have always been Nova. Thank you for being exactly who you are every single day without apology. Watching you navigate this world with joy and courage and complete authenticity is the greatest gift of my life. Every boundary I set, every truth I spoke, every morning I chose to get up and keep going, it was all for you. And it was all worth it.

To my mother, thank you for being Nana Rose. For the wisdom you passed down. For the sentences that became the spine of this entire series. You told me I was born knowing who I was. I am still learning to fully believe it. But I am getting closer every day.

To my little sisters and every young woman in my life, this series is for you. I wrote it so you would have something to hold in your hands on the days when the world tries to make you forget. You were born knowing. Never let anyone convince you otherwise.

To every neurodivergent girl who has ever been rushed in a hallway or made to feel like the way her body works is something to hide, Nova is for you specifically. Your stimming is not a flaw. It is your body taking care of itself. Honor it.

And to every girl who picks up this book in her hardest season

You are seen.

You are enough.

You are that girl.

Now go remember her.

Also by Kendra Tamika:

Remember Her

The moment a woman stops searching for power and realizes she already is it.

She Always Knew, For the girl ages 6 to 9

She Rose, For the girl ages 13 to 17

She Arrived, For the young woman ages 18 to 25

Bake It. Brand It. Sell It.

The Complete Guide to Building a Profitable Food Brand
From Home to Retail

www.ingramcontent.com/pod-product-compliance
Lightning Source LLC
LaVergne TN
LVHW010620110826
845149LV00003B/985

* 9 7 9 8 9 9 5 4 7 0 5 4 0 *